This book belongs to:

....

Copyright © 2014 Acamar Films Ltd

First published in the UK in 2014 by HarperCollins *Children's Books*,
a division of HarperCollins Publishers Ltd, 77-85 Fulham Palace Road, London W6 8JB

1 3 5 7 9 10 8 6 4 2

ISBN: 978-0-00-752981-0

Based on the script by Lead Writers: Ted Dewan and Philip Bergkvist and Team Writers: Lucy Murphy and Mikael Shields.

Adapted from the original books by Ted Dewan and using images created by Acamar Films, Brown Bag Films and Tandem Ltd.

Edited by Neil Dunnicliffe.

Designed by Anna Lubecka.

Bing™

Smoothie

HarperCollins Children's Books

Round the corner,
not far away,
Bing is having a snack today.

Hello
Bing.

Hello
Flop.

Bing and Flop are in the kitchen. It's **snack-time** for Bing.

Flop takes
a carrot.

He **spins** it,
throws it up
into the air...

and
catches
it!

Yum!

Bing **loves** carrots.

He takes a **big** bite.

CRUNNCH!

Bing **throws** the carrot in the air.

WHOOPS!

Where did it go?

There
it is!

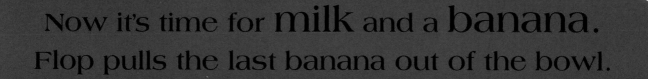

Now it's time for milk and a banana.
Flop pulls the last banana out of the bowl.

Oh dear, it's very ripe and very brown.

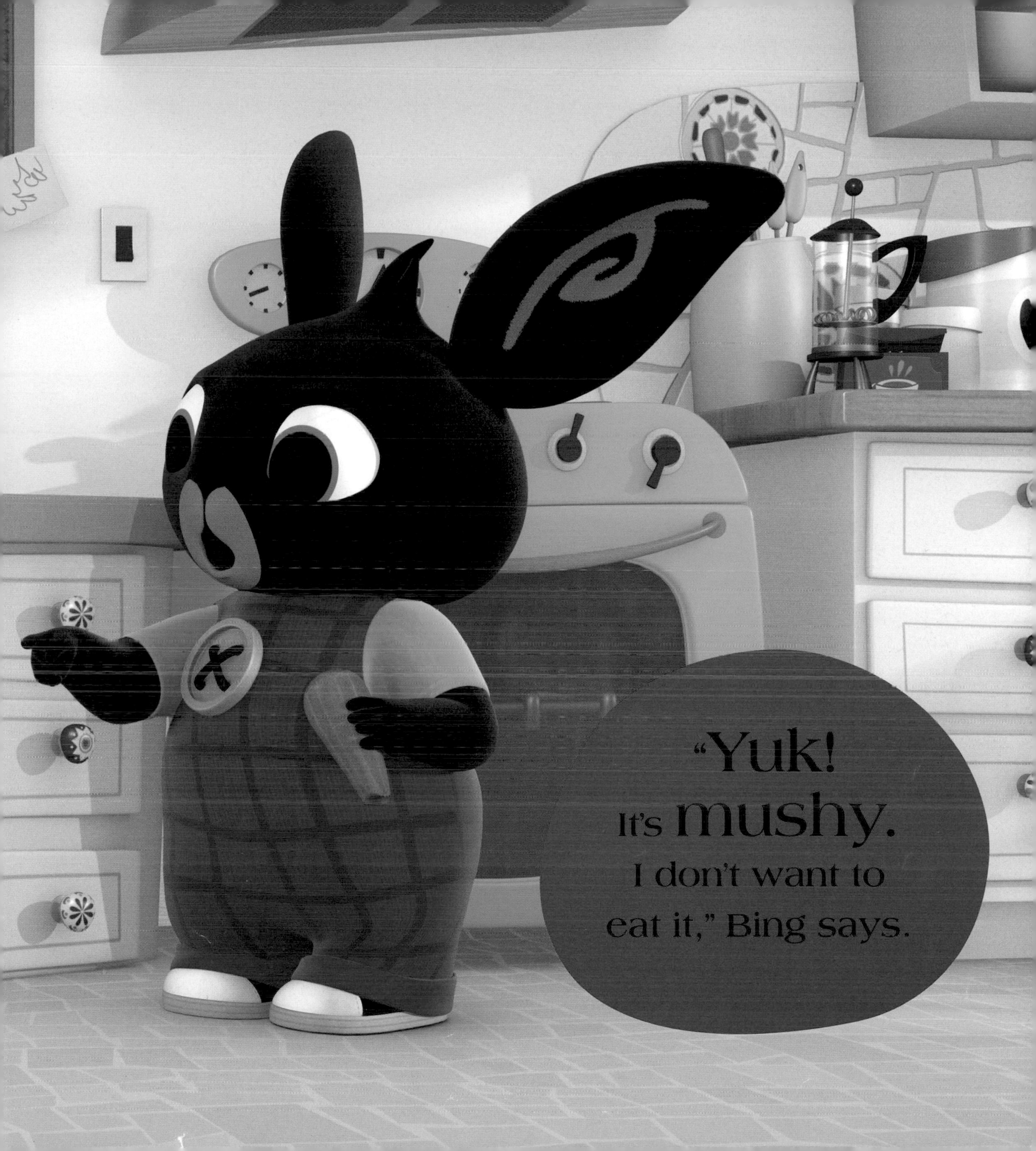

"Yuk!
It's mushy.
I don't want to
eat it," Bing says.

"Why don't we **drink**
the banana?" asks Flop.

"Silly Flop, you
can't **drink**
a banana!"
laughs Bing.

"You can't drink a banana?" says Flop as he brings in...

Brenda the blender!

"Brenda the blender. Food blender extra-ordin-aire. Let's make a smoothie," says Flop.

"Can I do **top speed?"** asks Bing.

"Sure. But first we have to **squish** the banana into the jug, fill the jug with milk, **mix it up** at low speed and then..."

"Top speed!" shouts Bing.

Bing **squeezes** the banana out of its skin.

"It's doing a poo!" he giggles.

PLOP!

PLOP!

PLOP!

It drops into the blender.

“Now let’s add the milk,” says Flop.

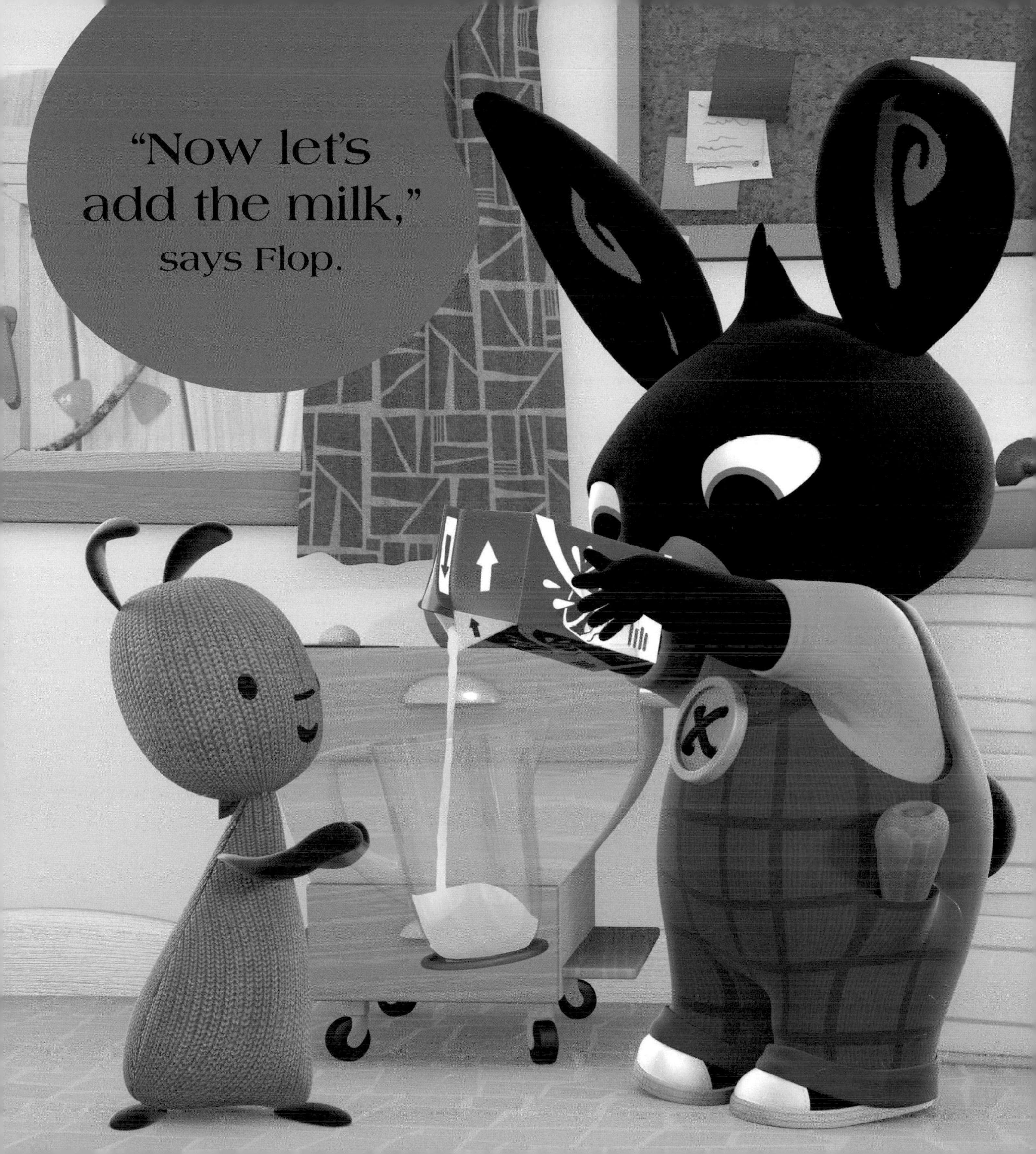

"Low speed first. To get the lumps out. If it's lumpy, you know what happens? Brenda goes

wubble, wubble, wubble!"

"Ok... let's go...go...go...go...go!"

Brenda mixes everything together.
"All the lumps are gone, but we need to add a
little more milk," says Flop.

Bing isn't listening. He's **throwing** his carrot.

WHOOPS!

Where did it go?

Flop adds more milk
to the blender and
puts the lid back on.

"OK, Bing.
Top speed?"
he says.

"Yup.
Top
speed!"
shouts Bing.

"Let's go...go...go...go...go!"

Brenda **shakes** and takes
a while to reach top speed.

Suddenly, Bing wonders where his carrot has gone.

Then he spots something inside the blender.

"Brenda's got
my carrot!"
says Bing. "I want
my carrot!"

Flop looks inside the blender. "I don't think your carrot is going to come back," he says.

"Whhhyyyyy?"
asks Bing.

"Because the **banana**,
the **milk** and your **carrot**
are all **mixed up together**.

Look!" says Flop,
"Brenda's made you
a **yummy carrot
smoothie**."

"Try it, Bing!"

Bing sips the
smoothie through
a straw.

"Aaahhh."

"Yum?"

"Ooh,
yum!"

"Good for you, Bing Bunny."

Hi!

My banana was all **mushy**.

So we put the **pooey** banana and the milk into Brenda, and Brenda **mixed** everything together.